P9-EKY-540

Red Parka Mary

written by Peter Eyvindson
illustrated by Rhian Brynjolson

PEMMICAN PUBLICATIONS INC.

CALGARY PUBLIC LIBRARY

Copyright © 1996 by Peter Eyvindson. All rights reserved.
No part of this work covered by the copyrights hereon may be reproduced or used in any form or by any means – graphic, electronic or mechanical – without prior written permission of the publisher Pemmican Publications. Any requests for photocopying, recording, taping or information storage and retrieval systems of any part of this book shall be directed in writing to the Canadian Copyright Licensing Agency, 6 Adelaide Street East, Suite 900, Toronto, ON M5C 1H6.

Illustrations Copyright © 1996 by Rhian Brynjolson.
All rights reserved.

Pemmican Publications Inc. gratefully acknowledges the assistance accorded to its publishing program by the Manitoba Arts Council and the Canada Council.

Printed and Bound in Canada

Canadian Cataloguing in Publication Data

Eyvindson, Peter

    Red parka mary

    ISBN 0-921827-50-4

1. Brynjolson, Rhian.   11. Title.

PS8559.Y95R4 1996   jC.813'.54   C95-920206-4
PZ7.E99Re 1996

PEMMICAN PUBLICATIONS INC.
Unit 2 - 1635 Burrows Avenue
Winnipeg, MB R2X 0T1 Canada

*For Dona and her character
Sophie whose real name is Mary.*
Peter

*For our "old folks", the stories they tell
and the patience they teach us.*

Sincere thanks to Virginia, June and Matthew.

*Thanks also to Frontier School Division
and Berens River School.*
Rhian

Chokecherry jelly and rabbit fur remind me
of Christmas and Red Parka Mary.

At first I was scared of her. She didn't hide behind the trees waiting to pop out and scare me. Nor did she ever try to chase after me. But there was something about her that scared me.

It might have been the way Mary dressed. It didn't matter if it was 40 below or 40 above, she always wore big floppy moccasins lined with rabbit fur, thick grey wool socks, three or four sweaters heavily darned at the elbow and a Montreal Canadien hockey toque pulled down over her straggly grey hair. She was missing four or five front teeth and her skin was brown and wrinkled. Yet, that wasn't what scared me.

I think it was because even though I was only seven, someone, somehow, sometime, had told me that because of her brown eyes, I should be frightened.

I couldn't help it. Every time I passed by her house, I would stare at her. Sometimes she would wave but every time that happened, I would get embarrassed, turn my head back to the road and rush off for home.

I must have done that for what seemed like years until the time I heard her call. It made me stop immediately. No one had ever called me Mister before.

"Hey, Mister." she repeated.

"Take these to your mom," she said as she held out a pail brimful of chokecherries. "I've got all I need."

I stood there in the middle of the road with my mouth hanging open, not moving and not knowing what to do. Mary eventually carried the pail half way, plunked it down on the edge of the road and shuffled back to her front door.

I didn't know what to do. Should I take them or should I leave them? Finally I decided that maybe Mom would know what to do with them.

She did. When that pail of chokecherries turned into jelly and ended up on the breakfast table, I decided that maybe Mary wasn't so scary after all.

Mom agreed.

"That Mary," she chuckled to herself. "I should have given her the whole bag of sugar instead of just lending her a cup."

The next morning I took Mary her pail filled with a bag of sugar. She smiled a toothless grin and patted me on the head.

For the first time, on the way home from school that afternoon, I stopped when she waved at me from her front step.

"Hi, Mary," I said.

"Hey, Mister!" she called. "Come here for a minute."

She held out a piece of warm freshly baked bread sprinkled generously with white sugar.

We sat on the top step and talked. Or at least she talked. I mostly listened.

I found out the reason why Mary wore those moccasins. Her bunions were so bad she couldn't wear shoes. And she wore four sweaters because that was all she owned. Only in the summertime did her four sweaters make her feel comfortable. In winter, unless she was baking bread, she was always cold.

She taught me how to snare a rabbit, how to skin it, how to thread a needle, how to make leather soft and supple, and finally, how to line my own homemade moccasins with rabbit fur.

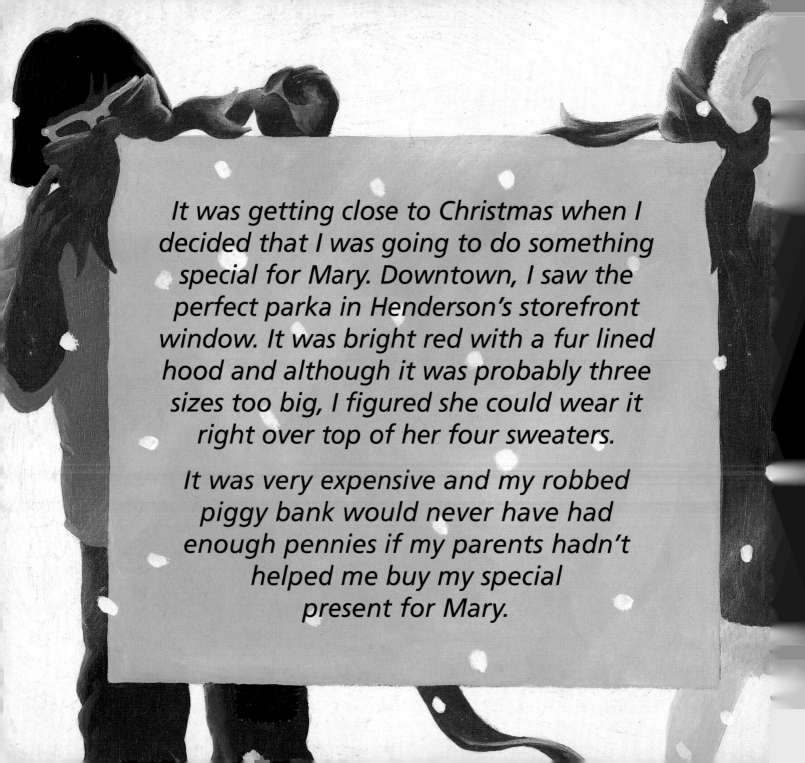

It was getting close to Christmas when I decided that I was going to do something special for Mary. Downtown, I saw the perfect parka in Henderson's storefront window. It was bright red with a fur lined hood and although it was probably three sizes too big, I figured she could wear it right over top of her four sweaters.

It was very expensive and my robbed piggy bank would never have had enough pennies if my parents hadn't helped me buy my special present for Mary.

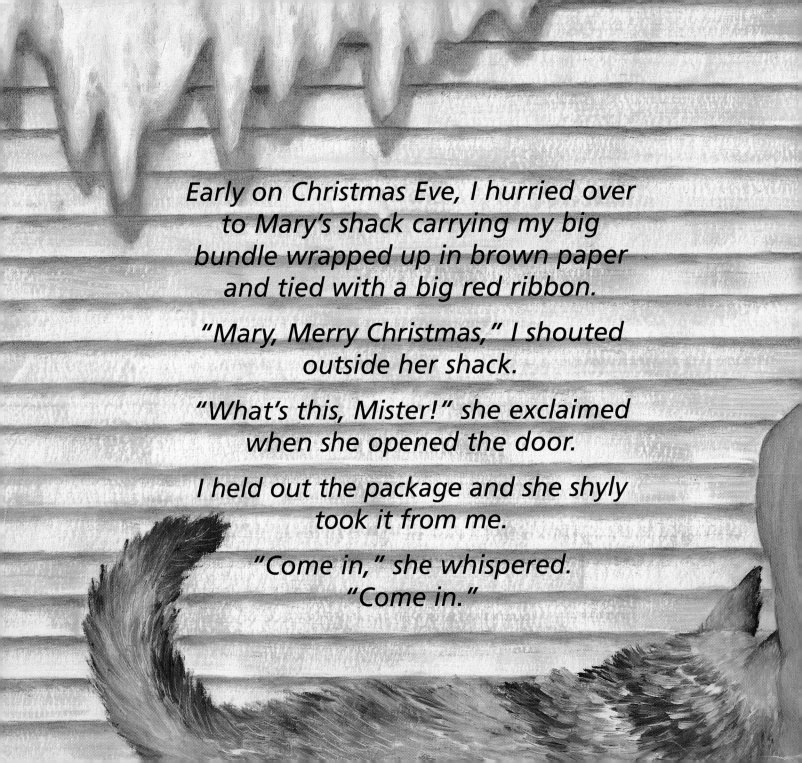

Early on Christmas Eve, I hurried over
to Mary's shack carrying my big
bundle wrapped up in brown paper
and tied with a big red ribbon.

"Mary, Merry Christmas," I shouted
outside her shack.

"What's this, Mister!" she exclaimed
when she opened the door.

I held out the package and she shyly
took it from me.

"Come in," she whispered.
"Come in."

Right in front of her wood stove she ripped off the paper and pulled out the bright red parka. Quickly she pulled it on over her sweaters and for a moment we stood awkwardly staring at each other.

Suddenly I was embarrassed because I hadn't thought that maybe Mary would feel that she should have a gift for me because I had brought her a gift. Yet I knew she would have nothing to give.

"M—mom says for me to ask you to come over for Christmas dinner," I stammered. "Four o'clock."

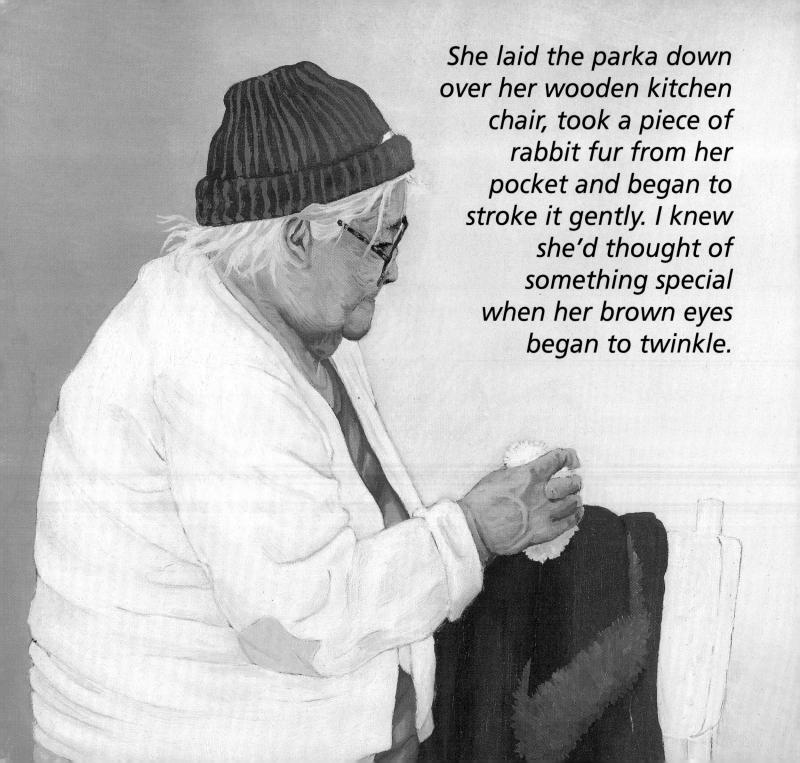

She laid the parka down over her wooden kitchen chair, took a piece of rabbit fur from her pocket and began to stroke it gently. I knew she'd thought of something special when her brown eyes began to twinkle.

"Hey, Mister!" she exclaimed. "Tomorrow I'm gonna give you the biggest gift in the whole wide world. Do you know what it is?"

"N—n-no," I stammered.

"Guess!" she exclaimed. "What is the biggest and best present in the whole wide world?"

"Um. A..a..castle?" I asked.

"No, no! Not now!" Mary interrupted. "Tomorrow for Christmas dinner, I'll bring it but you'll have to guess."

That night instead of wondering when Santa was going to arrive I wondered about Mary's special gift. What was the biggest and best thing in the whole wide world?

Scri

Name
_____

Scri

Nam

At four o'clock, even before Mary could knock on our door,
I threw it open and yelled:
"Is it as big as Buckingham Palace?"

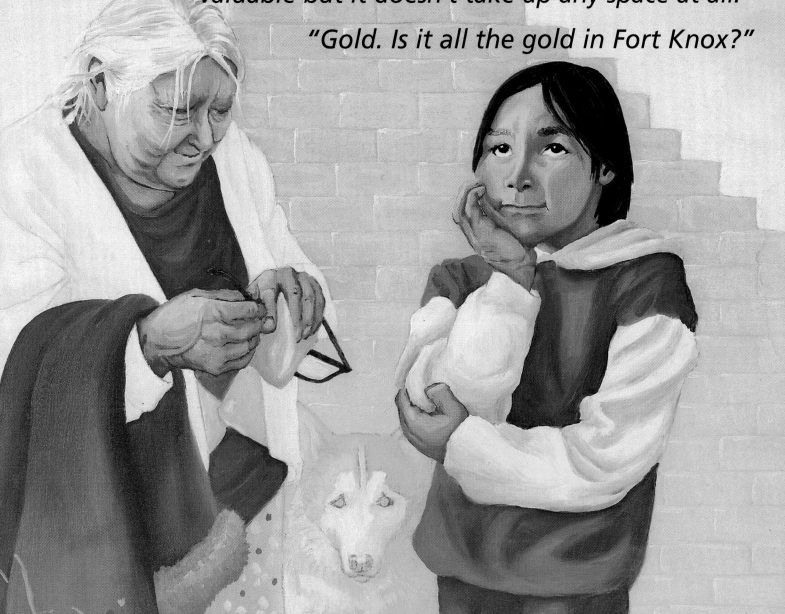

"Far bigger than Buckingham Palace!" Mary chuckled as she stepped inside and took off her new parka. "And far more valuable but it doesn't take up any space at all."

"Gold. Is it all the gold in Fort Knox?"

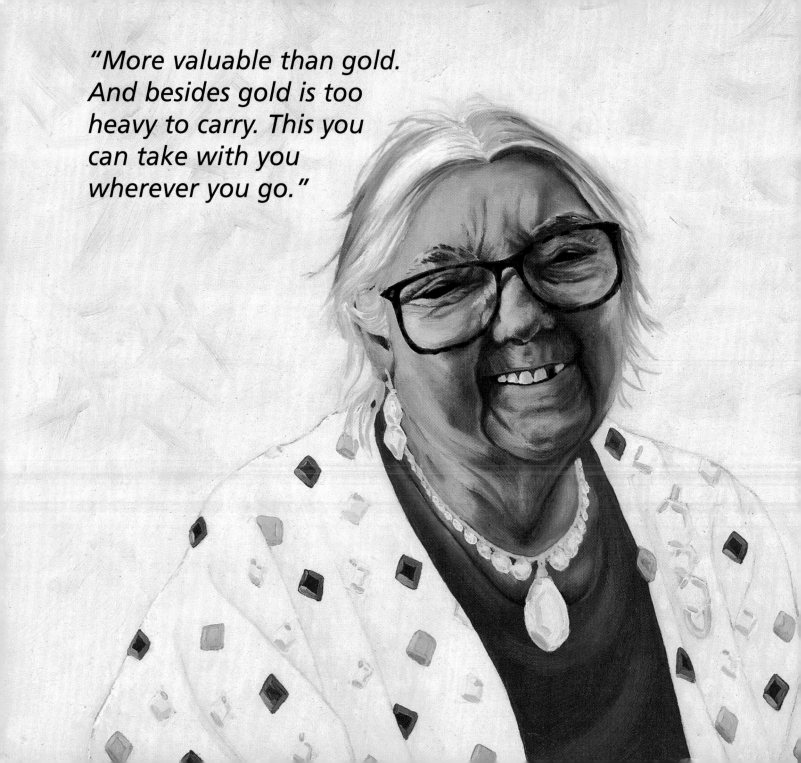

"More valuable than gold. And besides gold is too heavy to carry. This you can take with you wherever you go."

"Jewels. It must be jewels!" I exclaimed.

"No, it isn't jewels. Robbers like to steal jewels and this nobody can take from you."

She poked her hand into the pocket of her tattered old sweater and pulled out the smallest box I'd ever seen.

"Open it." Red Parka Mary demanded.

For a moment I held it wondering how this could be the biggest and best present ever. It wasn't big. Nor was it heavy.

When I took off the lid and looked inside the box, the contents didn't look very valuable either. I found a single small red heart-shaped bead laying on a bed of white rabbit fur.

"That little heart, Mister," she said softly, "stands for love. I can always give you love."

I took her love that day as she folded her grandmother arms around me and squeezed me tight. And it was then that I knew that I loved the way she dressed, her straggly grey hair, her missing teeth, her brown wrinkled skin and especially her eyes.

Yet I can't help but wonder. Why did someone, somehow, sometime, tell me to be frightened of those twinkling brown eyes?

Other Books by Peter Eyvindson

Chester Bear, Where Are You?

Circus Berserkus

A Crow Named Joe

Jen and the Great One

Kyle's Bath

The Missing Sun

The Night Rebecca Stayed Too Late

Old Enough

The Wish Wind

The Yesterday Stone

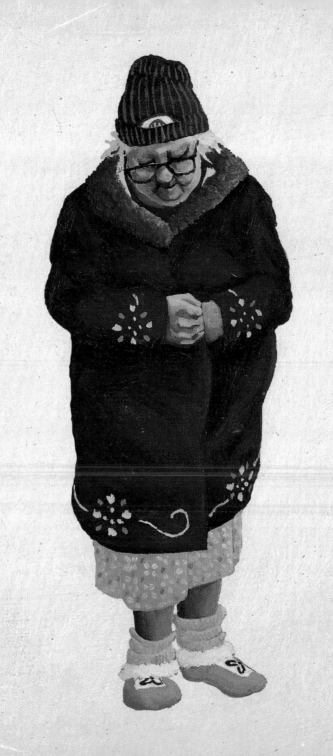